Ella Calista Wilson

The bachelor's Christmas

A Christmas Entertainment

Ella Calista Wilson

The bachelor's Christmas
A Christmas Entertainment

ISBN/EAN: 9783741193750

Manufactured in Europe, USA, Canada, Australia, Japa

Cover: Foto ©Andreas Hilbeck / pixelio.de

Manufactured and distributed by brebook publishing software
(www.brebook.com)

Ella Calista Wilson

The bachelor's Christmas

THE

BACHELOR'S CHRISTMAS

A CHRISTMAS ENTERTAINMENT

BY

E. C. W.

AUTHOR OF "SANTA CLAUS AT HOME"

———————

BOSTON

GEORGE M. BAKER & COMPANY

REMARKS.

THIS little play is written for the use of persons wishing at Christmas some very simple entertainment which a few can execute, and which will be short, easy of performance, and inexpensive. Do not be afraid to select and trust quite young children to do their parts. The author has had much experience with young children, and they always more than fulfil expectations. Work easily and quietly with them, and do not rehearse them too much. Instruct them to speak clearly, loudly, and slowly. Never, no matter if the speech be of but one word, let them hurry; and always make a good opportunity for their little speeches, and give them *time* enough to have full effect. A child young enough to sit in a high-chair, and be given a rattle and other playthings, will add very much to the picturesqueness of the piece, and will give good opportunity for grouping and occupying the other children. The child may be called "baby," even if quite old, if it is somewhat small.

DRAMATIS PERSONÆ.

MR. ROBERT CHESTER. — A wealthy, hot-tempered, but kind-hearted bachelor.

MRS. WILTON. — A poor widow with a family of small children. She proves to be Mr. Chester's sister.

HARRY. — Mrs. Wilton's oldest child.

REX, DAISY, DOTTY, and BABY. — Her other children.

A serving-boy.

HARRIET. — A maid.

COSTUMES.

MR. CHESTER always as comfortably and stylishly dressed as is possible.

MRS. WILTON and the children very poorly, with clothing neat but patched, until the last scene, when they must be gotten up to look as pretty and stylish as possible.

Time, less than an hour.

PROLOGUE.

(Before the curtain. Enter DAISY *and* DOTTY: *trip to the middle of stage.)*

DOTTY.

Merry Christmas! Merry Christmas!
  Merry Christmas to you all!
Merry Christmas, fathers, mothers;
Merry Christmas, sisters, brothers;
  To big folks and to small.

DAISY.

We can wish it, *you* must make it.
  In the *heart* the merry grows:
From the heart the face must take it,
  Till with Christmas joy it glows.

DAISY *and* DOTTY.

So Merry Christmas! Merry Christmas!
  Merry Christmas to you all!
Merry Christmas, fathers, mothers;
Merry Christmas, sisters, brothers;
  To big folks and to small.

4

A BACHELOR'S CHRISTMAS.

SCENE I.

Street. Two days before Christmas. Enter MR. CHESTER. He is muffled up very warm and comfortable looking.

MR. CHESTER (*searching for something on the ground*). Fool! Idiot! To lose a pocket-book at my age! I must be getting into my dotage. Br-r-r! How cold it is! A curse on the malicious fates! I shall never see that money and those valuable papers again. You can stake your — (*Stops suddenly on looking up, and seeing HARRY watching him. HARRY's clothes are patched; he has no overcoat; a tippet around his neck. He has his hands in pockets, and keeps his feet in motion to keep them warm.*) Hullo, youngster! What are you spying after, I should like to know? Haven't you any thing better to do than to stand around poking fun at your betters?

HARRY. I'm not poking fun, sir.

MR. C. Well, just let me know why you constitute yourself a spy on gentlemen's movements. Hey! Get out of my way, I say, young impudence (*lifts his*

5

cane threateningly at him. HARRY *dodges*). What do
you want around here, anyway?

HARRY. I thought you seemed to be looking for
something, sir.

MR. C. Well, and if I was looking for something?
Isn't that my privilege, sir? Be off, I say! (*Suddenly
changing tone, as an idea strikes him.*) I say, little
boy, you haven't found any thing, have you?

HARRY. Yes, sir: I found a pocket-book with a lot
of money in it.

MR. C. (*irritably*). Well, now you talk business.
(*Angrily.*) But why don't you give it to me, and not
stand gaping there? I suppose you want to chaffer
about the reward. Hand it over, I say! (*Strikes the
ground angrily with his cane.*) Hand it over. You
need have no fears. I shall pay you handsomely.

HARRY. But mother said I was to be sure it was
the right man, 'cause there's ever so much money in it.

MR. C. True. Your mother is right. Of course,
of course. But I *am* the right man, you see: so you
may give it to me.

HARRY. But mother said I must ask the man his
name; for there's a whole bunch of his cards in it.

MR. C. Why, of course! What a dolt I am!
I'm acting like the impatient idiot that I am, and the
boy keeps his temper like a gentleman. (*Bending down
pleasantly to* HARRY.) My name is Robert Chester.
Now, is that the name in the pocket-book?

HARRY. Yes, sir; that is the name.

MR. C. Well, then, now you will give me the
pocket-book, won't you, like a nice little boy?

HARRY. But I haven't got it.

MR. C. Fury and lightning! Haven't got it! Then where in — Ah-ahem (*bending pleasantly down to the boy again*). Where is it, then, my little man?

HARRY. Mother's got it. She says I'm too little to carry around such a lot of money. I'll go right home and get it. (*He starts to go.*)

MR. C. That's true, of course. Your mother is right again. Here, wait. I'll give you my card, so your business-like mother will be satisfied (*puts his hand in overcoat-pocket for his pocket-book, then suddenly recollecting*). Oh, I forget! my cards are in my con— Ah, in my lost pocket-book, you know, of course. Here (*he finds a scrap of paper in one of his pockets, writes his name on it, and gives it to* HARRY). There, that will do. How far do you live?

HARRY. Just around the corner. I'll be back in two jiffies. (*He runs off.*)

MR. C. (*solo*). Now, I wonder how long the chap will be gone. I haven't half-a-dozen wits about me, or I should have gone with him. Br-r-r! How cold it is! Ah, here comes the boy! He's spry, that's a fact. One *must* be, this weather, or freeze. (*Enter* HARRY, *out of breath.*) See here, youngster, are you crazy? Don't you know it's cold weather?

HARRY (*staring in surprise*). Sir!

MR. C. I say, it's a stinger of a day. Why don't you wear your overcoat?

HARRY. I haven't any overcoat. I've got this big tippet, though.

MR. C. Nonsense! Now, what a reasonable yarn

that is! Haven't any overcoat, such weather as this! That's likely, *that* is. Why doesn't your stupid father get you one?

HARRY (*a little proudly*). I haven't any father, and my father *wasn't* stupid.

MR. C. I beg your pardon. Of course he wasn't. (*Aside.*) I'm the stupid one. No father at all! that's shocking really, and such a baby too! (*To boy.*) But aren't you cold, you know?

HARRY. A little bit, sometimes; but when I'm big I'll earn me an overcoat.

MR. C. (*aside*). Hear him, now! D'ye s'pose he's too *poor* to have a coat? On honor, I've heard them tell of such things; but no, it's absurd, it can't be. Not to have an overcoat, such weather as *this!* (*To boy.*) Well, little boy, did you bring my pocket-book? If you did, I'm thinking you've earned yourself an overcoat without waiting till you're big.

HARRY. Mother says she is sorry to trouble you, sir; but I'm not very big, and, as it's only a step, she would feel safer if she gave it to you herself.

MR. C. Bah! another delay. I was a fool not to go with you in the first place. After all, she is right. Come along, my man. (*Exeunt* MR. CHESTER *and* HARRY.)

SCENE II.

Mrs. Wilton's *home.   Very poor and desolate looking. The pocket-book lies half-open on a pine table.   The children, excepting* Harry, *gathered around the table, intent upon the pocket-book.* Mrs. Wilton *aside, holding in her hand the piece of paper* Harry *brought from* Mr. Chester.

Rex.   Oh my buttons!   Just look, Daisy!   See the *piles* of money.   My eyes!   I wish it was ours.   We'd have the big turkey that's hanging up down to Smith's for Christmas dinner, wouldn't we though?   'n' cran-b'ries, 'n' nuts, 'n' all the fixings.   (*They peep at it excitedly, but do not touch it.*)

Mrs. W. (*apart, looking at the paper in her hands*). Robert Chester! my own brother.   And this was writ-ten by his own hand!   What will he be like?   (*Greatly agitated.*)   Will he know me?   No, no, he will not know me.   Twelve long years of poverty have changed me so!   How I tremble at thought of meeting him again!

Daisy (*going to her mother*).   Mamma, would you know how to cook a great big turkey?

Rex.   'Cause if you would, mamma, keep the money, 'n' we can buy the one hanging up down to Smith's, 'n' have some more coal, 'n' be warm.   Keep it, mother: *I* would.   Harry found it, 'n' *I* think it's ours.

Mrs. W.   Hush, dears: you do not know what you are saying.   The money isn't ours.   Hark! they are coming. (*Aside.*) Heaven help me! I tremble like a leaf.

(*Steps outside.* HARRY *rushes in, runs up to his mother, and speaks hastily.*)

HARRY. He's cross as a bear, mother, but don't you be afraid. He's all right. (*Rushes back, shows in* MR. CHESTER.) Mamma, this is Mr. Chester. He's the man who lost the pocket-book.

MR. C. (*very much embarrassed*). Your son, madam, ahem — your boy here — ahem! (*He looks in wonder around the room.*) You don't mean to say, madam, that you live here!

MRS. W. Yes, sir: this is our home. (*Aside.*) He doesn't know me! It is cruel — cruel!

MR. C. But really, madam (*still looking around*), ahem — I beg your pardon, it's none of my affairs, you know; but — ah — well, ahem — ah — What I mean is, you know, I shouldn't think you'd like it.

MRS. W. (*aside*). Poor Robert! He's no idea of poverty. How should he have? He has always lived in luxury. (*To* MR. CHESTER.) It's the best I can do for them, sir. My family is large, and I have no husband and no money.

MR. C. Hm! Really! Possible! I'd no idea, you know, it was so bad. We give a good deal of money to 'em for the poor; really we do indeed, madam, and you ought to have some of it. Of course you ought. Hm! (*Excited.*) It's shocking you haven't. It is really, you know.

MRS. W. (*aside*). My own brother, and he *will* not know me. And *he* has changed too. It seems impossible that this is my bright brother Bob.

Mr. C. And your boy found my pocket-book. I am the right man, madam. Indeed, you may believe me.

Mrs. W. (*giving him the pocket-book*). Certainly I believe you, and I am very glad my son was able to do you the service.

Mr. C. Yes, yes. And what shall I — you know what I mean — ah — What's the right thing to pay him for his honesty, you know? How much do you want?

Mrs. W. (*proudly*). We want *no* pay, sir, for being honest. Honesty is its own reward.

Mr. C. (*nervously*). Why, yes, of course, madam; of course, without doubt. That's a very sublime sentiment, — very, and I approve of it perfectly, perfectly, madam; (*turning to* Harry) but look here, young man, you know, set your own price, and you needn't be at all bashful.

Harry. Mother is right. I will not be paid for being honest.

Mr. C. (*striking his cane angrily on the floor*). Confusion to your fine sentiments! You little simpleton, I say you *shall* be paid. Gods and heroes! Do you think you're to do me a service like that, and not be paid for it? (*The children start back when he strikes his cane, the smallest one clinging to its mother.*)

Daisy (*coming forward in front of* Mr. Chester, *and stamping her little foot vigorously, and looking up in his face*). Harry isn't a simpleton, and you're a naughty, bad man. Harry sha'n't take whatever he don't want to — *so* now! (*Stamps again.*)

MR. C. (*frowning down at* DAISY *a moment, then upon all the rest, suddenly bursts into a laugh*). Ha, ha, ha! You pretty baby! What do *you* know about it, — *you?* See here, baby, wouldn't you like a lot of money? now say, *wouldn't* you?

DAISY. 'Nuff to buy the big turkey hanging up down to Smif's?

DOTTY. 'N' some candy dogs 'n' horses?

REX. 'N' me a big tippet like Harry's?

MR. C. That's it exactly, my cherubs: you've hit it plum. And your little fool of a brother won't take the money. Now, what do you say to that?

DAISY (*stamping again*). Harry isn't a fool-ver-brover, and if Harry doesn't want us to have 'em we don't want 'em. (*Wags her head at him defiantly, and goes to* HARRY.) Won't you let the man give us some money? *Please* do, Harry dear, and we'll have a nice big fire, and be warm. It's cold.

MR. C. (*winces as he looks at the fire*). Shades! It's only the ghost of a fire.

DOTTY. An' we'll be rich, Hally.

REX. *Do*, Hal. Let him. We need the money more'n he does.

HARRY (*to* Mr. CHESTER). When I found your pocket-book, sir, I was going over to do some errands for Smith. He was going to give me half a dollar. I lost the job waiting round for you. You could pay me the half-dollar, if you please, sir, — just for my time, you see.

MR. C. Ha, ha! You are a regular little business man, *you* are. Really, I like that, after all. And what were you going to do with your half-dollar, pray?

HARRY. Mother and I were going to get some little presents to put in the children's stockings.

MR. C. (*very much amused*). The *children's* stockings! That goes ahead of every thing yet. And aren't you one of the children yourself, pray?

HARRY. Oh, yes! but I'm the big one, you know; and — and father told me to help mother take care of the littler ones.

MR. C. (*aside, very much affected*). And what could you buy for the little ones, my man, with your fifty cents?

HARRY (*brightly*). Oh, lots of things! A tippet for Rex; and there's lots of cunning little things for the girls at Carter's, for only five cents apiece; and then some candy, (*hastening to explain*) just the very least bit, you know, sir, to tuck way, way down in the toes.

MR. C. Well, my boy, here's your fifty cents (*giving him a silver half-dollar*); and you've earned it, my boy, indeed you have (*brushes his eyes excitedly*). You are a good boy, a *very* good boy. (*Turning to* MRS. WILTON ; *the children all examine* HARRY's *half-dollar.*) Madam, you ought to be proud of your son: he's a man, every inch of him. I'm a cross, crusty old bach ; but I've got half an eye, and I can see they are fine children, all of 'em. And now, madam, be kind enough to take this money (*lays a bill on the table*), and buy them some nice Christmas presents. (MRS. W. *makes a motion of refusing.*) No, no, my dear madam !

it is not to pay your honesty; no, indeed (*pompously*), certainly not. It would be absurd, it would be an insult, to offer anybody pay for being honest, — ahem (*embarrassed*), ah — ah — of course it would. I agree with you. It's only a Christmas present to your good little children; just exactly, madam, just exactly as I would give Christmas presents to my little nephews any nieces if I had any. Yes — ah — that's it; I agree with you perfectly, you know.

Mrs. W. (*aside*). Oh, it is cruel! Why *will* he not know they *are* his nephews and nieces? I will tell him. (*Starts to attract his attention, but her courage fails.*) No, no, I cannot: I have not the courage. It is enough just to have seen his dear face: I will be satisfied.

Mr. C. Good-day, madam. (*To* HARRY.) Good-day, my fine boy. Good-day, all of you. A — a — merry Christmas; yes, merry Christmas, that's the way they say it, and I trust you'll have it. You'll hear from me again, madam; yes indeed, of course. I wouldn't let it end there. Good-day. (*Exit.*)

Mrs. W. My brother! my brother Bob, and he is gone, actually gone! It is too cruel! I cannot bear it. I was wrong, I was wrong! I should have told him. He is hasty, but he is not hard-hearted. He would have taken care of my little ones; and now he is gone, and I know not where. (*Buries face in her pocket-handkerchief. The children gather, some about baby, some about* HARRY *and his money.*)

(*Curtain.*)

SCENE III.

Mr. Chester's *room in hotel. Enter* Mr. Chester *in his costume of Scene I. and II.*

Mr. C. (*throws his gloves on the table with an emphatic gesture*). Really, I wouldn't have believed it. It doesn't seem possible, such poverty as that. Right under our very eyes, too! Well (*proudly*), I've always given them all the money they've asked me for, for charitable purposes, — every cent. I've never been grudging. It's a comfortable reflection, that is, — a *very* comfortable reflection. (*Hangs his overcoat on the nail while talking, then takes off his boots, and puts on slippers. He takes off his inside coat, and in an absent-minded way throws it into the corner of the room, and tries to hang his boots on the nail.*) Well, really! What an old dotard I'm getting to be! Here I am hanging up my boots, and throwing my coat in the corner. (*He puts them right.*) Strange I cannot get these people out of my mind! I didn't believe I had such a thing as a heart. I thought it was dried and withered all to nothing. And here I find I have one, and it is stirred through and through. Bah! I'm getting weak and feminine. I sent them the turkey. I'll send them fifty or a hundred dollars, and forget all about them. Really, it's absurd to allow myself to be so weak. (*Rings the bell, and, picking up a paper, seats himself to read. Enter boy. He takes no notice. Boy waits respectfully. Looks up.*) Dolt! Don't you see those boots? Well, and haven't you eyes to see that they need blacking? (*Exit boy with boots.*) My mind reverts continually to Mary. My pretty sister Mary! Perhaps she is alone in the world like this woman, — alone and poor, with half a dozen children to care for. God forgive me! I was a beast to turn her away because she married a poor man, — I (*blubbering*), I who was all she had after father and mother died. What a beast I was! I'm a criminal. I'll give myself to the authorities to be hung. (*Blows his nose, and paces the stage excitedly.*) What weakness and folly is this! (*Fiercely.*) It was her own fault. What *right* had she to marry a man without a cent in his pocket? I gave her her choice, — her own brother, or poverty. She chose the poverty, — she freely and deliberately chose the poverty. It is her own fault — not mine. (*Seats himself savagely in a chair, and tries to read. A few notes of piano in an adjoining apartment are heard, then a voice sings, "*Peace on earth, good-will to men,*" etc. Throws paper angrily down. Singing continues.*) Thrum, thrum, thrum! They are at that eternal rehearsal again. I suppose they will keep that up till after Christmas (*pacing excitedly up and down the stage*). No one ought to be allowed to disturb people's peace in this fashion. If they must keep up such a racket, they ought to be made to get off by themselves. (*Sits down, and gradually begins to listen. Song stops. A few lingering notes on the piano.*) "Peace on earth, good-will to men!" I know I shall never know peace on earth again till I find my sister Mary, and find her I will. (*Gets up excited again,* *pounds the table with his fist.*) When Robert Chester says he will do a thing, it is done; and before Heaven I say I will find her! Marry a poor man, indeed! Why should she not marry a poor man if she chooses? I admire her pluck for doing it. Wouldn't I marry a poor woman if it pleased my will? Bast! (*Soberly and with great feeling.*) But poor Mary! Perhaps she is like this woman—who knows? How do I know her husband is still living? Twelve years! He's had time enough to die a dozen times. But (*vehemently pounding the table with his fist*) I say I will find Mary. I'll—I'll—I'll be her slave. (*Blubbers. Enter boy.*)

Boy. Did you call me?

Mr. C. (*angrily*). Did I ring?

Boy. You pounded, sir.

Mr. C. (*fiercely*). Well, hasn't a man the privilege in this hotel of pounding without being called to task for it? Go! (*Exit boy.*) But how to find my poor Mary? I have it! I'll advertise. (*Picks up piece of paper, takes pencil from pocket, and writes "Lost."*) Lost, lost! No, that won't do (*crosses it, and writes again*). Strayed, strayed! I should say she was a cow (*crosses it out*). I'm an idiot. I'll employ a detective. No, that's worse yet. I should hope she isn't a thief or a murderer. (*Throws down pencil, scowls, and thinks a moment. Suddenly starts up in great excitement, and rushes up and down the stage.*) Know-nothing! Fool! Idiot! No wonder the voice thrilled me! No wonder my dead heart came to life again! It's Mary. It's Mary herself! Heaven forgive me! Have I let her come to this? I did not know; I—I

— how should I, — how *should* I know it was so bad? But no, no, it isn't Mary. It can't be! Mary was rosy and plump and beautiful; and this woman — But twelve years! Twelve years of *such* living! No wonder she is changed! (*Flies around excitedly.*) But I'll get her — I'll get her and her children this instant. (*Looks for his boots, and rings bell.*) Strange she did not know me, — very strange! (*Blubbers.*) And I'll be a father to her children. I'll— (*Enter boy.*) You scoun — (*Aside.*) Wait! If I'm to be a father to Mary's babies, I must stop that sort of thing. (*Aloud to boy.*) I say, will you please be kind enough to bring me my boots? and (*fiercely*) mind you are not half an hour about it either. (*Exit boy.*) This Christmas will find me a changed man. (*Puts on his overcoat energetically.*) What a wretch I've been! What a blind-eyed, crusty old cosseter of myself I've been! But it's ended. I— (*Enter boy; he puts down boots, looks shyly at* Mr. Chester, *and exit.* Mr. Chester *sits down, and tries to put on his boots.*) I'm an old — old — I never knew before a man couldn't put on his boots with his overcoat on. (*Throws off overcoat, puts on boots very rapidly, draws on mittens, puts on hat. and picks up cane*). I always thought Christmas was a regular bore, but I believe I'm getting on a thorough Christmas spirit myself. (*Cutely to audience.*) Send 'em fifty or a hundred dollars, and forget them! ha, ha! I made a joke that time, didn't I? Ha, ha! (*Exit smartly.*)

SCENE IV.

Mrs. Wilton's *home.* *A big turkey lying on the table.*
The children gathered around the turkey in delight.
Mrs. Wilton *sitting thoughtfully apart.*

Harry (*pulling the turkey by one leg, the better to examine it*). It *is*, it's the big turkey that was hanging up at Smith's. I know him sure: I've looked at him so *many* times, wishing we could have him.

Daisy. And now we've got him!

Rex. Who do you s'pose sent him?

Daisy. That man, *of course.*

Harry. Oh! but he's a fat fellow. My eyes! I wish he was baked.

Mrs. W. (*aside*). He's a kind man if he *is* gruff. I wish I had had the courage to tell him I am his sister. He is rich. Perhaps he would have taken care of us. Oh, my poor husband, my poor dear husband! (*Puts her head on the table, with her face in her handkerchief. The children go toward her.*)

Daisy. Mamma, dear mamma, what is it? Please tell us. Aren't you glad we've got a turkey, and lots of money? Don't, mamma dear, don't cry. We were so poor yesterday, and now we are rich.

Rex. Say, mamma, *are* we rich now? and what makes you cry?

Harry. *I* know. She is thinking of papa. I've been thinking of him too. But mamma (*anxiously*) it'll be Christmas in two days, you know; and oughtn't we to make it as merry as we can, — just for the children?

Mrs. W.   Just for the children!   You dear, brave, tiny little man!   How would mamma ever get on without *you*?   (*Takes* Harry's *face between her hands, and kisses it.*)   Yes, we *will* make it merry.   You must all hang up your stockings to-morrow night, and I don't believe Santa Claus will forget you.   To-morrow afternoon you will be good children, and take care of the house ; and I will go down town, and spend (*holds up finger merrily at them*) — *you* know what!   (*Children dance, and clap their hands.*)   And it will all be secret ; and you must shut your eyes when I come home, and not ask any questions.   And then Christmas morning! ah, won't our eyes shine!   You'll see!   (*Children dance, and clap hands.*)

Harry.   *I* ought to go with you to carry the bundles, mamma.   (*A knock, and* Mr. Chester *enters.* Mrs. Wilton *starts.*)

Mr. C. (*looking very stern*).   Well!   (*He looks around the room.   Aside.*)   How shall I begin?   It's very embarrassing.   (*He scowls.*)   Well!

Mrs. W. (*aside*).   How he scowls, and how stern he looks!   Oh, he suspects, and he is angry!   Now Heaven help us!

Daisy (*stepping in front of him, and looking up in his face*).   Was it you 't sent it?

Mr. C. (*taking no notice*).   Bad enough! bad enough! I can hardly believe my senses.   (*Aside.*)   Yes, it is my sister, my beautiful blooming sister Mary.   (*Aloud.*)   And you say you have no father?

MRS. W. No, they have no father. Their father died nearly a year ago.

MR. C. (*suddenly and in a commanding tone, rapping his cane on the floor*). But I say they *have* a father. (*Pauses grandly. The children seem a little frightened.*) I say they *have* a father. Now and in the future *I* am their father so long as I live. (*Pauses again in an impressive manner.*)

DAISY (*stepping forward, stamping her foot, and looking up in his face*). You're *not* our papa. You sha'n't be our papa. Our papa wasn't cross. He was kind and good, — *ever* so kind and good. (*Steps back, wagging her head defiantly.*)

MR. C. (*frowning down at* DAISY, *then around at the rest. He breaks down stammering and blubbering*). Mary, Mary, my sister, don't you know me? don't you know your brother Bob? (*Blows his nose, and is very much excited.* MRS. WILTON *buries her face in her handkerchief, and sobs.*)

REX (*fiercely, stepping toward him belligerently*). You go away! You are a naughty, bad man, 'n' you make my mother cry.

HARRY. And take your turkey, and all your money.

DAISY (*going in front of him, and stamping*). Go away!

DOTTY (*going in front of him, and stamping*). Quick, *or fie* quick!

MR. C. (*dreadfully perplexed*). See here, Mary, your children are afraid of me. Tell 'em, tell 'em, Mary: *I* can't. Tell 'em I'm their father. — See here now, children, you know, I'm not cross. Really, now,

little dears, I'm not. I'm the kindest man in this city;
I am now, really, only — why, you see, I don't know
how to show it. (*Suddenly winks to audience triumph-
antly. Aside.*) I have it! (*Sits down, and ogles to
the children, and beckons to them.*) Come here now,
little dears, and I'll tell you a story, — a *true* one!
Come now.

DOTTY (*coming over to him*). And won't you hurt
us — truly?

MR. C. No, indeed. (*Puts her on his knee.*)
There, I like that! You shall be my especial pet.
Now (*to DAISY*), you come too, little pussy. (*Makes
a noise as if calling a cat.*)

DOTTY (*putting her hand on his cheek, and pulling his
face toward hers*). Daisy isn't a kitty.

MR. C. (*feigning the greatest surprise*). No indeed!
There, now I have you. (*The boys draw nearer.*) Now
for the story. (*Very pompously, and as though it were
an astonishing statement.*) Once I was a little boy no
bigger than you!

REX. O' course.

DAISY. *All* big folks was little folks like us once,
wasn't they?

MR. C. (*puzzled and aside*). What *shall* I say next?
How *shall* I tell 'em? I *won't* tell 'em at all: they'll
hate me. I'll patch it up somehow. (*Aloud to the
children.*) And I had a little sister, — a dear, beautiful
(*blubbers, and takes out handkerchief*), beautiful little
sister. It was your own mother, children, — your own
mother, my beautiful, rosy little sister was. Mary (*turning to her*), Mary, come here, and tell them it is true.

Mrs. W. (*rises, and stands beside* Mr. Chester *with her arm over his shoulder*). Yes, my darlings, it is my own dear brother Robert; and thank God he is come!

Mr. C. (*using his handkerchief freely*). And, children, it's a big world — and — and — and I lost her. And now I've found her, and I shall never lose her again. (*Gets up, and very clumsily puts his arms around her, and kisses her.*) No indeed, I will never lose her again, before Heaven I swear it! (*To the children, in his ogling tone again.*) And now, little darlings, will you let me be your father?

Dotty. If you'll be good.

Daisy. And if mamma says so.

Mr. C. *If* and *if!* It seems, then, I may get the mitten yet. Hey, little folks, I have a fat pocket-book, you know; and you won't have to wish for things any more and not have them — ha, ha! How will you like that?

Rex. And shall we drive a span, and have lots of servants, and live in a castle?

Mr. C. Hi! (*very proudly and grandly*) my son, you get on fast.

Daisy. Like kings and queens in fairy stories? (*Claps her hands.*) Oh, I shall *love* that!

Mr. C. (*proudly again*). Tut, tut, my little daughter! Your expectations tally with your brother's, don't they?

Mrs. W. (*smiling*). No, no, dears, not that. Your uncle means plenty of food, and warm clothing to keep you warm, and — and — a happy, comfortable home.

Mr. C. (*looking grandly around on the company*).

Am I, then, at last the accepted head of this house, and father of these children?

REX (*running to him, and taking his hand*). Oh, you good, good, new papa!

DAISY (*she and DOTTY clinging to his other hand; baby with mamma*). I'll be good always, *always*, and mind you; and I *know* I'll like to be rich.

MR. C. Tut, tut!

DOTTY. An' me too.

HARRY (*throwing his arms around his mother's neck*). O mother, mother! It's too good.

MR. C. (*raising his finger at* HARRY). And mind, I'm to have no rival. You have no further charge of these little ones. You are to be my (*proudly*) eldest son, and one of the babies.

(*Curtain falls with finger still up.*)

SCENE V.

Handsome parlor of the new home. MRS. WILTON *making one or two ribbon bows at the table.*

MR. C. (*pacing up and down the stage, rubbing his hands delightedly*). I tell you, Mary, we were lucky to get this all furnished at so short notice. Here it's been standing idle for four months. I believe it was just waiting for us. And to think they made me pay two hundred more for it on account of the children! Ha, ha, ha! Really now, I never knew before, — I really didn't, — that the little rabbits were so much below par. But just let 'em try to get *mine* (*proudly*) away, — let 'em try it *that* way, and they'll find 'em at rather a heavy premium : eh, Mary?

Mrs. W. (*snips off end of ribbon, and throws down work*). Yes, brother, we *were* fortunate in getting the house. And, Robert, you don't know it, but it was very quick work getting the children fitted out as you wished ; but I hope you will find them to your liking.

Mr. C. I trust so — I trust so. But, Mary my dear, (*pompously*) the nephews and nieces of Robert Chester ought to have every thing that is needful in the way of dress. (*Rings for servant; comes over to his sister's side.*) And to think, Mary (*pulls out his handkerchief*), that my own sister should have been poor and homeless with all her little ones, and I—I— (*blubbers*) I rolling up a great bank account — boo-hoo — all for myself — for one cosseted, crusty, snarly, withered-up old bach. It's shocking, it is really, you know. But I'll be a good father to your children, Mary. Really, I will, Mary. I— (*Knock, and maid enters. Wipes eyes hastily, straightens up majestically, and goes toward the maid.*) Harriet, you understand the children are to be here at seven. And mind you, (*getting excited*) seven doesn't mean quarter *of* seven nor quarter *past* seven — but *just* seven precisely and exactly. (*Exit maid.*)

Mrs. W. Robert, if you wish to be a good father to the children —

Mr. C. I know. I know. I go off like a fire-cracker. But (*proudly*) I shall stop it, — I shall stop it for the children's sake. (*Very pompously.*) If I'm to govern this house and these children, of course I must govern myself. That's it — that's it; and I shall do it, too. (*Knock, and re-enters maid.*)

MAID. If you please, sir, is baby to be brought in with the other children?

MR. C. (*in a fury*). Is baby to be brought in with the other children! And what would you do with baby, pray, if he isn't brought in with the other children? Tell me that, if you please. Would you throw him out of the window? Would you —

MRS. W. (*placing her hand on his arm*). Robert dear —

MR. C. Yes, Mary my dear, there I go again. (*To maid, very politely.*) Harriet, my love, you may bring baby in with the other children, certainly. And, my love, (*very mysteriously*) keep them in the nursery till seven, then bring them here. Prompt at seven, you understand, my love. (*Exit maid, eying* MR. CHESTER *quizzically.*) There, sister Mary, that's a good beginning, you'll own. You mustn't despair of me. You see, my heart is so bursting full of Christmas peace and love and good-will, that it — why, you know what I mean — it will break out in spite of me.

DAISY (*behind scenes*). I won't stay in that old room. I'm going in that pretty room with mamma.

REX (*same*). No, you mustn't. Our new papa said we mustn't.

MRS. W. Robert dear, I think I'll go myself, and look after the children till seven o'clock. Harriet will never be able to control them. (*Exit.*)

MR. C. (*rubbing his hands in delight*). Our new

papa! Now, really, that means me, you know. It
does, really. Of *course* Harriet will not be able to
control those children. They are bright children, those
children of mine are. *Nobody* will be able to control
them,—nobody except myself (*with great importance*),
and I shall rule them solely by love; solely by love,
that's it. Ha, ha, ha! Won't the fellows at the club
die with envy when they see me at the head of this
house and all these children? Oh, but it will be sport
to see them! it will now, really. But (*looking at his
watch*) they will be here in a few minutes. This
won't do. I must get to work (*picks up a Santa
Claus costume lying on sofa*). I made a monkey of
myself once to be Santa Claus, but that was when I
was young. Bah! After all, I'm not so old *now;* no
indeed, I'm a young man yet. How does this thing go
anyhow, I wonder? (*Dresses as he talks.*) Now, that
is a gay ticket. I wonder if the little rabbits will know
me. I rather guess! You can't blind *those* young-
sters very easily! (*Puts on wig.*) They *will* be 'cute
if they know me now. (*Turns round and round before
the glass, and admires himself delightedly.*) Ha!
Won't their eyes shine, though! (*Puts a big bag over
his back, and hangs a pair of skates, a trumpet, a tin
horse, two dolls, and other toys over him.*) There!
I'm a festive-looking Santa Claus, at all events.
(*Voices outside,* "Here, wait for me, Rexie!") Here
they come, bless 'em! (*Enter* DAISY.)

DAISY (*peeps in, coming far enough to be well seen.
At sight of* SANTA CLAUS, *holds up both hands in amaze-
ment, and exclaims*). Oh, my! Oh! (*Rushes off the*

stage screaming very loudly.) Harry, Harry! Rex!
All of you! Come quick! It's Santa Claus! Really
and truly Santa Claus, right here in our parlor! Where
did he go? (*Enter the children. They look all about
expectantly.*)

HARRY. Nonsense, Daisy, you little goosie! you're
fooling us.

REX. Pooh! Santa Claus *never* comes right out
like that.

DAISY. But I saw him! I saw him alive! Right
here! With my two eyes! (*Dancing around, and
hunting for* SANTA.)

DOT. Course she did! Daisy wouldn't tell a lie.
I'll find him.

ALL THE CHILDREN (*spying him*). Oh, there he is!
Oh, my! It *is* Santa Claus, as true as you live!
(*Clap their hands, and dance up and down during these
exclamations.*)

SANTA (*coming out and frisking around*). Well,
little folks. a merry Christmas to you all!

ALL. Merry Christmas! Merry Christmas! How
did you get here? Oh, but isn't he jolly! (*They clap
hands and dance around.*)

DAISY (*going up to him*). Are you the truly, truly
Santa Claus? Honest?

HARRY. Of course he is.

REX. You can see that with one eye.

ALL. Oh, my! Isn't it fine! (*Clap hands, and
dance around* SANTA.)

HARRY. See those skates! Oh my eyes!

REX. My buttons! and that drum! (DAISY *and*

DOTTY *whisper together, and point to the dolls. Enter mamma with youngest child, if very small, in arms.*)

CHILDREN. O mamma! It's really and truly Santa Claus! (SANTA, *who all this time has been frisking around, and shaking the presents teasingly at the children, begins to take them off. He holds up the skates.*)

SANTA. Now, here's a fine pair of skates! They are just the thing for — for — let me see — for the baby.

CHILDREN. The *baby!* (*They laugh.*) No, no — no *indeed!* They'll just fit Harry. (*In the scramble for the skates,* DAISY *or* DOTTY, *if big enough, gets the skates, gives them to* HARRY, *giving him at the same time a hug around the neck.*)

SANTA. And these dolls! (*Rocks them to and fro, singing "By-low-baby."*) I do believe Rex here has his eye on these dolls! (*Laughter again.*)

CHILDREN (*boisterously*). You funny, naughty Santa!

REX. A boy have dolls!

HARRY. You must give Daisy and Dotty the dolls.

DOTTY. Of course. (SANTA *gives dolls to the little girls.*)

SANTA. And here's just the prettiest drum I could find in my toy-shop. Daisy and Dotty will want that too, I suppose. (*Children, laughing boisterously, scramble for the drum, and hang it over* REX'S *neck. They pull the toys from* SANTA, *he pretending to defend himself. One or two toys like a jumping-jack, a ball, and perhaps a few handfuls of candy,* SANTA *tosses slyly to the children in the audience. The children on the stage get among the toys some bonbons; each snaps one, and puts one of the paper caps on. Rex laughingly puts one on baby, and Daisy on her mother. Daisy then steps off, and exclaims with a wag of her head.)* There!

Santa. There, children! Now, hasn't old Santa treated you handsomely? (*He holds up his finger for them to keep quiet, and pulls from his pocket a gold watch and chain. Goes to mamma, and fastens the chain around her neck very proudly and affectionately.*) And see what we have for dear, dear mamma!

Children. Oh! (*Admiringly.*) Oh! You dear, dear old Santa Claus! Oh, you jolly old darling!

Santa (*takes baby in arms*). And now, my dear, dear little folks, what is the very best of all the Christmas presents Santa Claus has brought you?

Children. Our new papa! Our beautiful, splendid new papa!

Santa. And the very, very best Christmas gift he has brought to your new papa is a big, precious family to love and to care for. And so (*coming forward in centre*) God bless us all, and give us every year —

Mrs. W. A merry Christmas and a bright New Year.

Rex. And send us Santa loaded down with toys.

Harry. And fill our hearts with merry Christmas joys.

Daisy. And *we* will help to make the Christmas merry —

Dotty. By being kind and loving, very, very, *very*. (*Music strikes up. Santa puts baby on the floor in*

front at one of the sides, takes Mrs. Wilton *as part-
ner; the children pair,* Rex *with* Daisy *and* Harry
with Dotty, *and dance around the stage.*)
(*Curtain.*)

Note. — After the curtain, Santa may go down into
the audience, and distribute boxes of candy or bonbons to the
children. It would be a good way, to have Santa Claus,
when he is distributing the presents to the children in the
play, toss to some gentleman in the audience boxes of candy
or bonbons. They may be kept until now, and he can now
distribute them. Santa may stay around in his costume
as entertainer-in-general as long as is desirable.

You will find the Piece you are looking for among 60 of the Choicest
Selections in the

No.3 Reading Club and Handy Speaker.

Edited by GEORGE M. BAKER.

Price, cloth, 50 cents; paper, 15 cents.

CONTENTS.

If you are looking for Something New, you will find it among
50 of the Choicest Selections in the

No. 4 Reading Club and Handy Speaker

Edited by GEORGE M. BAKER.

Price, cloth, 50 cents; paper, 15 cents.

CONTENTS.

*Sold by all booksellers and newsdealers, and sent by mail, postpaid, on
receipt of price.*

LEE & SHEPARD, Publishers, Boston.

No.1 Reading Club and Handy Speaker.

Edited by GEORGE M. BAKER.

Price, cloth, 50 cents; paper, 15 cents.

CONTENTS.

Sold by all booksellers and newsdealers, and sent by mail, postpaid, on receipt of price.

LEE and SHEPARD, Publishers, Boston.

No. 2 Reading Club and Handy Speaker

Edited by GEORGE M. BAKER.

Price, cloth, 50 cents; paper, 15 cents.

CONTENTS.

LEE & SHEPARD, Publishers, Boston

No.7 Reading-Club and Handy Speaker.

Edited by GEORGE M. BAKER.

Price, cloth, 50 cents : paper, 15 cents.

CONTENTS.

LEE & SHEPARD, Publishers, Boston.

No. 5 Reading Club and Handy Speaker

Edited by George M. Baker

Price, cloth, 50 cents; paper, 15 cents.

CONTENTS.

No. 6 Reading Club and Handy Speaker.

Edited by GEORGE M. BAKER.

Price, cloth, 50 cents ; paper, 15 cents.

CONTENTS.

LEE & SHEPARD, Publishers. Boston.

No.9 Reading-Club and Handy Speaker.

Edited by GEORGE M. BAKER.

Price, cloth, 50 cents ; paper, 15 cents.

CONTENTS.

Sold by all booksellers and newsdealers, and sent by mail, post paid, on receipt of price.

LEE & SHEPARD, Publishers, Boston.

Acknowledged the Best.   50 of the Choicest Selections in the

Nº 10 Reading-Club and Handy Speaker.

Edited by GEORGE M. BAKER.

Price, cloth, 50 cents ; paper, 15 cents.

CONTENTS.

Sold by all booksellers and newsdealers, and sent by mail, post-paid, on receipt of price.

LEE & SHEPARD, Publishers, Boston.

No. 11 Reading-Club and Handy Speaker.

Edited by GEORGE M. BAKER.

Price, cloth, 50 cents; paper, 15 cents.

CONTENTS.

www.ingramcontent.com/pod-product-compliance
Lightning Source LLC
Chambersburg PA
CBHW020817030726
47496CB00009B/2923